For my mom, Patti Tracy (aka River Ames), the first writer in the family —K.T.

For Mom and Dad, because of the picky days of my childhood when
all I wanted to have to eat was toast with strawberry jam —E.K.

Farrar Straus Giroux Books for Young Readers
An imprint of Macmillan Publishing Group, LLC
120 Broadway, New York, NY 10271
mackids.com

Our books may be purchased in bulk for promotional, educational, or business use. Please contact your local bookseller or the Macmillan Corporate and Premium Sales Department at (800) 221-7945 ext. 5442 or by email at MacmillanSpecialMarkets@macmillan.com.

Library of Congress Cataloging-in-Publication Data
Names: Tracy, Kristen, 1972–author. | Kraan, Erin, illustrator.
Title: I am picky : confessions of a fussy eater / Kristen Tracy ; pictures by Erin Kraan.
Description: First edition. | New York : Farrar Straus Giroux, 2022. | Audience: Ages 3–6. | Audience: Grades K–1.
| Summary: A young raccoon who claims to be a picky eater tries to fill his ferocious appetite as he makes his way through trash cans and compost bins.
Identifiers: LCCN 2021045005 | ISBN 9780374389543 (hardcover)
Subjects: CYAC: Raccoon–Fiction. | Food habits–Fiction. | LCGFT: Picture books.
Classification: LCC PZ7.T68295 Iam 2022 | DDC [E]—dc23
LC record available at https://lccn.loc.gov/2021045005

First edition, 2022
Book design by John Daly
Color separations by Embassy Graphics
Printed in China by Hung Hing Off-set Printing Co. Ltd., Heshan City, Guangdong Province

ISBN 978-0-374-38954-3 (hardcover)

1 3 5 7 9 10 8 6 4 2

I AM PICKY

CONFESSIONS of a Fussy Eater

WRITTEN by
KRISTEN TRACY

Pictures by
Erin Kraan

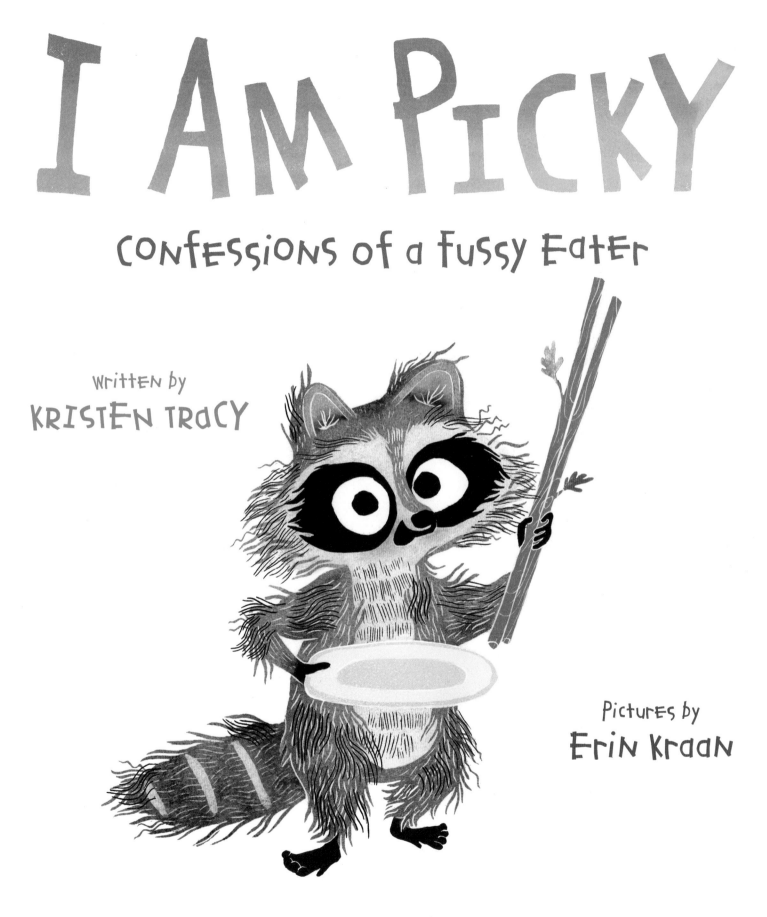

Farrar Straus Giroux
NEW YORK

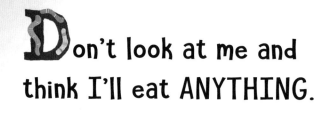

Don't look at me and think I'll eat ANYTHING.

I will NOT. I am PICKY.
I've been choosy my whole life.

My mom's picky.

She ONLY eats fish heads when they're attached to their bony spines.

My dad's picky.

SQUIRT!
SQUIRT!
SQUIRT!

He NEVER nibbles on chewy snacks
without plenty of mustard.

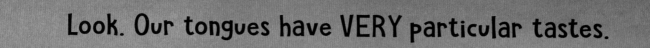

Look. Our tongues have VERY particular tastes.

Is it tough being this picky? TOTALLY!

You've got to
reach deep into
the pond scum.

You've got to dig all the way to
the bottom of the compost bin.

CRUNCH.
CRUNCH.

Tender morsels don't just fall from the sky.

Except when they do.

Some things only taste good together.
Like bright flowers and crunchy bees. *Nom. Nom. Nom.*
MAGNIFIQUE!

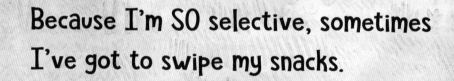

Because I'm SO selective, sometimes
I've got to swipe my snacks.

CRUNCH.
CRUNCH.

I am a special breed. I WANT what I WANT.

No matter which den I leave, finding
the right snack is always a challenge.

I consider myself a seasonal eater.
Nothing tastes better than a fresh
harvest meal.

chef's kiss!

BURP!

Ugh. Do you see what I see? Yuck. Blech.
Snails. I AM SO PICKY. Don't think you'll
ever catch me eating a snail.
I will NOT.

Choosy as I am, I actually have a favorite snack.

It's tastier than berries, nuts, insects, small fish, eggs, moldy bread, muskrats, vegetable gardens, tropical fruit, and garbage—COMBINED.

This breakfast treat requires my sneakiest move.

ZOOM!

What can I say? I'm lucky. My mom's lucky.
And my dad's lucky too.

That's what I call a
successful snacking spree.
BRRRP
GARLIC BREAD

Wait. Oh no! Where are my manners? I've eaten all these snacks and haven't offered to share anything. Let's see what I can put together.